Tales of Amazing Maidens

★

For our dear bold God daughters:

Charlotte Rose and Heid-Maria
P.C.
Lilly, Lola, Ruth and Nina
S.H.

Pomme Clayton would like to thank:

Georgiana Jerstad for her unique version
of *Anansi's Daughter* (and for allowing
me to write it down).

Pamela Marre for her help and invaluable
editorial comments.

Jacques Nimki for his patient reading
of so many different versions,
and constant support.

Laura Simms for her telling of *Delgadina*,
which was one of the sources
consulted while writing the story.

★

Orchard Books
96 Leonard Street, London EC2A 4RH
Orchard Books Australia
14 Mars Road, Lane Cove, NSW 2066
Text © Pomme Clayton 1995
Illustrations © Sophie Herxheimer 1995
ISBN 1 85213 792 4
First published in Great Britain 1995
A CIP catalogue record of this book is available
from the British Library.
Printed in Belgium

Tales of Amazing Maidens

Retold by Pomme Clayton

Illustrated by Sophie Herxheimer

ORCHARD BOOKS

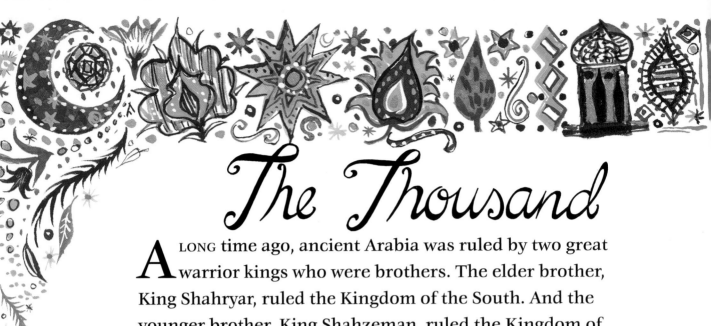

The Thousand

A LONG time ago, ancient Arabia was ruled by two great warrior kings who were brothers. The elder brother, King Shahryar, ruled the Kingdom of the South. And the younger brother, King Shahzeman, ruled the Kingdom of the North. They reigned fairly and both kingdoms flourished.

Many years passed, and the brothers did not see each other. Then King Shahryar sent a messenger to the Kingdom of the North, inviting his brother to stay. King Shahzeman was delighted, and he prepared for the journey at once. Camels were loaded with food and water and tents. When everything was ready, King Shahzeman kissed his wife goodbye, and the camel train headed into the desert.

They travelled all morning, but by noon it was so hot that even the camels were gasping. So the party stopped beside an oasis, where servants made sweet mint tea and everyone rested in the shade. Then Shahzeman realised he had left something at home. It was a box decorated with rare jewels that he wanted to give to his brother. So he ordered the party to set up camp and returned for the box.

King Shahzeman took his fastest camel and thundered back to the palace. When he arrived it was getting dark, and

he went straight to the royal apartments. As he searched for the box, he heard laughter from the bedroom. He opened the door, and there was his wife in the arms of another man. They were kissing.

King Shahzeman went wild with rage. "No sooner have I left my kingdom," he shouted, "than you betray me!" Then he drew the sharp scimitar from his belt, and slashed off his wife's head.

The King told no one of what he had seen or done. He returned to the oasis, and the camel train continued on its journey. But Shahzeman's heart was so heavy he did not even notice if it was day or night.

When King Shahzeman arrived at the Kingdom of the South, his brother was overjoyed to see him. A huge feast was given in his honour, but Shahzeman ate nothing. King Shahryar asked him what was wrong, but Shahzeman said nothing. Shahzeman could not even give his brother the beautiful box, for it was bursting with bad memories.

One day King Shahryar said, "My dear brother, come hunting with me, it might help you forget your troubles."

But Shahzeman refused. So Shahryar went hunting alone, while Shahzeman sat on a shady balcony overlooking

a small garden. He put his head in his hands and wished that the whole thing had never happened. He watched King Shahryar's wife walking in the garden when suddenly he saw a young man step out from behind a tree, and take the Queen into his arms. They laughed, then kissed each other.

King Shahzeman shuddered, "How cruel," he whispered, "that exactly the same thing should happen to my brother. I am not the only one to be betrayed. For my brother's sake, I will try to be happy."

So when King Shahryar returned from hunting, he found his brother feasting.

"Ah, my brother," cried Shahryar, "you are enjoying yourself at last. Tell me, why were you so sad?"

"Do not ask," begged Shahzeman.

"But I am your brother, please tell me."

"I found my wife in the arms of another man," Shahzeman said in a low voice. "I cut off her head in a fit of rage."

"This is dreadful news," said Shahryar. "But if it happened to me, I would do the same as you. Tell me, brother, why are you now so happy?"

"Do not ask," begged Shahzeman.

"But I am your brother, please tell me."

"Today I saw your wife in the arms of another man," he

murmured. "I am not
the only one to be betrayed."

King Shahryar went wild with rage. He ran to his
chamber, drew the sharp scimitar from his belt, and
slashed off his wife's head. Then he said to Shahzeman,
"Brother, now I have done the same as you."

The two brothers wept.

"We can never trust a woman again," said Shahryar.
"Each night let us marry a new wife, and chop off her head
in the morning."

The brothers grasped each other by the hand, and
promised to keep this terrible vow.

The next day Shahzeman returned to the Kingdom of
the North to fulfil his promise while King Shahryar ordered
his prime minister, the Vizier, to find him a new wife. That
night Shahryar was married, and the next morning he drew
his scimitar and slashed off his young wife's head.

Each day the Vizier had the miserable job of finding that
night's bride. One by one, all the maidens
in the city were married to the King.
And one by one they were all killed.
Mothers and fathers were terrified
that it might be their daughter next.
Families left their homes and
businesses, and fled. Everyone
hated the King. And the
Vizier hated his

job. He was desperate to find new brides for the King, because, if he couldn't, he knew the bride would have to be one of his own daughters.

The Vizier had two daughters, and he loved them more than anything. Since his wife had died, he had brought them up on his own. There was little Dunyazad, who was just a child, and Shaharazad, who was a bold and graceful maiden. Shaharazad loved stories, and every night she would light a candle, and tell her sister one of the wonderful stories she had heard in the marketplace, about speaking horses, demons, and magic carpets. These stories had taught Shaharazad a thing or two, and she began to think of a plan to save the kingdom from the King's terrible vow.

One evening the Vizier came home to find Shaharazad waiting up. "Father," she said, "I have a favour to ask."

"You know I would refuse you nothing," replied her father.

"Then marry me to the King."

The Vizier was horrified, "I could not do that."

"Father, please. I know I can save the kingdom from this terrible evil."

"Never!" cried her father.

"Well, if you won't offer me to the King, I will offer myself!"

Shaharazad had made up her mind, and the Vizier knew there was nothing he could do.

The next day she prepared for

the wedding. She put on her mother's beautiful wedding dress, and Dunyazad braided her hair.

"I need your help, Dunyazad," said her sister. "When I have been married to the King, I will call for you. I want you to say: 'My dear sister, please tell me one of your marvellous stories so that this dark night may pass happily.' Then, with the King's permission, I will tell a story. And with God's help, I will save the kingdom. Will you do that for me?"

Dunyazad nodded her head, and put the final touches to her sister's dress.

Shaharazad was married to King Shahryar, but it was not a happy event. There was no celebration, and there were no guests. Then Shaharazad was taken to the King's chamber, and she put her plan into action.

"Your Majesty," she said, "would you permit me to say goodbye to my sister?"

The King agreed and Dunyazad was brought to the chamber. She hugged Shaharazad and said, "My dear sister, please tell me one of your marvellous stories so that this dark night may pass happily."

Shaharazad turned to the King. "Only if Your Majesty allows . . ." she said gracefully.

"I like a good tale," said the King, "and I need distracting from my troubles. Begin!"

"Once upon a time, a long time ago," Shaharazad said softly, "there was and there was not . . ."

The King and Dunyazad listened, and the story came to life in their minds' eye. Shaharazad's voice transported them to the shore of a sea. They saw a fisherman, a genie, a talking fish and a king who was turned to stone! They were taken on an adventure, full of magic and unexpected twists and turns. But when Shaharazad got to the most exciting part, the sun rose, and she stopped speaking.

"Ohhh!" cried the King. "You can't stop there!"

"I only tell stories when it is night," said Shaharazad. "But what you have heard is nothing compared to what comes next."

The King longed to hear the rest of the story. "Very well, finish the story tonight," he ordered. "I will kill you tomorrow."

Then the Vizier appeared with tears rolling down his cheeks. He was carrying a winding sheet to wrap his daughter's dead body in, and was very surprised to find her alive. Shaharazad winked at her father, and he knew not to ask any questions.

That evening, Dunyazad said, "Please, Sister, finish the story."

Shaharazad continued with the adventure, and the King and Dunyazad listened enthralled. Shaharazad told so skilfully that before the story had ended another one had begun. She told them the story of Sinbad the sailor and his incredible voyages. But when Sinbad was just about to be swallowed by a whale, dawn broke and Shaharazad fell silent.

"What happens next?" pleaded the King.

"I only tell stories when it is night," said Shaharazad firmly.

"But I must hear the end!" cried the King.

"Finish the story tonight. I will kill you tomorrow."

Night after night, the King and Dunyazad listened to the stories. And night after night, the King wanted to know what happened next. Stories led into stories, that led into stories. Each morning the Vizier appeared with the winding sheet, expecting to find his daughter dead, but each morning she was still alive.

And so the stories went on for a thousand nights. Shaharazad told them of Ali Baba and the magic cave of treasure, of the everlasting slippers that would not go away, and of the three wishes that went horribly wrong. She wove tales, spun stories and embroidered lies, until the stories spread out like a magnificent carpet, each a different coloured thread, glittering with its own light.

Then, on the thousand and first night, Shaharazad told a tender tale of love. She reached the end of the story, and this time she did not start a new one. She fell silent. Outside, the round moon shone brightly; it was still night. Shaharazad sat and waited. But the King said nothing, and a deep silence fell upon the room. At last Dunyazad, who was no longer a child but a young maiden, spoke. "Now, sir," she said, "will you cut off my sister's head?"

The King hung his head in shame. "Oh, Shaharazad," he said quietly, "I could never kill you. I have listened to you for a thousand and one nights, and I could listen to you for a thousand more. Your stories have taught me what love and wisdom truly are. You have freed me from my madness. Now I long to live, and to make up for all these years of horror. Can you ever forgive me?"

Shaharazad took the King into her arms. "There is nothing to forgive," she whispered, hugging him tight. "You are not the same man."

Dunyazad threw her arms around them both, then went out of the room. She returned carrying three babies and presented them to the King. "These are your children, Your Majesty. They were born during the thousand and one days!" The King looked in amazement at his children. And when dawn broke, the Vizier arrived, and he was so happy that he fainted!

Then King Shahryar sent a messenger to his brother, to give him the good news and invite him to stay.

When King Shahzeman arrived, he saw how Shahryar's life had been changed, and he renounced his vow. A huge party was given for Shaharazad. And King Shahzeman and Dunyazad fell in love, so the party turned into a wedding. There was feasting and dancing. But most of all, storytelling, in honour of Shaharazad, the greatest storyteller of all, who saved her life, and that of her people, by telling stories.

King Shahryar proclaimed that the stories must never be forgotten. So everyone in the land learned the stories. They were passed from mother to son, and from father to daughter, all the way down through time. And it is said that anyone who tells or hears even one of Shaharazad's stories will be blessed forever.

The Three Spinners

O NCE there lived a Girl who was very, very lazy. What she liked to do best of all, was . . . nothing!

One day her Mother found her curled up beside the fire. "Get a move on, girl," she complained. "There's work to be done; cooking and cleaning, chopping up firewood and fetching water." And she pointed at a basket of flax. "What about this flax? It's not going to spin itself."

"I wish it would," mumbled the Girl.

"What did you say?" roared her Mother.

"I said, it will have to spin itself, because I'm not going to do it. I hate spinning."

This was just too much, and her Mother gave her a stinging slap.

"Oouch!" shrieked the Girl, and began to cry.

Just at that moment, the Queen was passing by in her carriage. She heard the crying and wanted to know what was wrong, so she knocked at the cottage door.

"Oh, Your Majesty," said the Mother, curtseying. "We were not expecting you."

"Whaaa!" cried her daughter.

"Be quiet, girl," hissed her Mother, "it's the Queen."

"I hope no one is ill?" enquired the Queen.

"Oh no, Your Majesty," said the Mother, feeling very embarrassed.

"Whaaaaaa!"

"It's my daughter," admitted the Mother.

"Did you hit her?" asked the Queen.

"Well . . . um . . . I just had to." The Mother began to think very quickly indeed. "My daughter loves spinning, you see. She would spin from morning to night, if she had the chance. We only have one basket of flax, and she wanted to spin it all. I had to hit her, or we would have had no flax left."

"Is that so?" replied the Queen. "If she loves spinning, she must come and live with me. I have three huge rooms full of flax just waiting to be spun."

The Girl was called at once, bundled into the Queen's carriage, and whisked off to the palace.

When they arrived, the Girl was taken up a steep spiral staircase to the three rooms. The first room had flax all over the floor, and an old spinning wheel in the corner. The second room had flax piled halfway up the walls. The third room was so tightly packed with flax that the Queen didn't dare open the door in case it fell on top of them.

"Now, my dear," beamed the Queen, "if you can spin these three rooms of flax in three days, then you can marry my son." And she glided down the stairs, leaving the Girl alone.

Well, do you think the Girl wanted to marry the Queen's son? Of course she did! So she set to work right away.

"Spinning can't be that difficult," she said to herself as she sat down at the wheel.

Now I don't know if you have ever tried to spin, but it is not as easy as it looks. The Girl picked up a stalk of flax.

It was hard and coarse like string. She tapped her foot on the treadle, to turn the wheel, but the wheel went round backwards. She tried to twist and pull the flax in her fingers, like she'd seen her mother do. But it got into a terrible tangle and the dry fibres snapped. The flax cut her hands until they bled. With that, she kicked the spinning wheel over and began to cry.

"I will never spin all this flax in three days," she sobbed.

Then she heard a voice.

"Are you in trouble, girl?" it croaked.

She looked around and couldn't see anyone.

"Do you need some help?" said the voice again.

She went to the window and peered out. What a sight met her eyes, and it was not Rumpelstiltskin! For there stood three of the strangest old ladies she had ever seen in her life.

The first had one foot like yours or mine. But the other foot was like a flat frying pan, and came crashing down with every step she took. The second had one top lip like yours or mine. But the bottom lip was as large as a dinner plate, and hung down over her chest, swinging to and fro. The third had one thumb like yours or mine. But the other thumb was like a great red swollen balloon.

"What's the matter, child?" they asked.

"If I can spin three rooms full of flax in three days," sniffed the Girl, "I can marry the Queen's son. But I couldn't do it, even if I had three hundred years."

"What luck that we should come by. We are the Three Spinners and we love spinning, don't we, Sisters?"

The three old ladies nodded at each other.

"But you don't get something for nothing, do you, Sisters?"

The three old ladies shook their heads.

"What do you want then?" asked the Girl.

"We want to be invited to your wedding. We love weddings don't we, Sisters?"

The three old ladies nodded.

"But you must welcome us as your most important guests, and call us your dearest aunts."

"Is that all?" cried the Girl. "That's easy! Come in, come in."

The Three Spinners climbed the staircase. Then one with the big foot sat down at the spinning wheel and tapped her foot on the treadle. The wheel went round, in the right direction, so fast you couldn't see it.

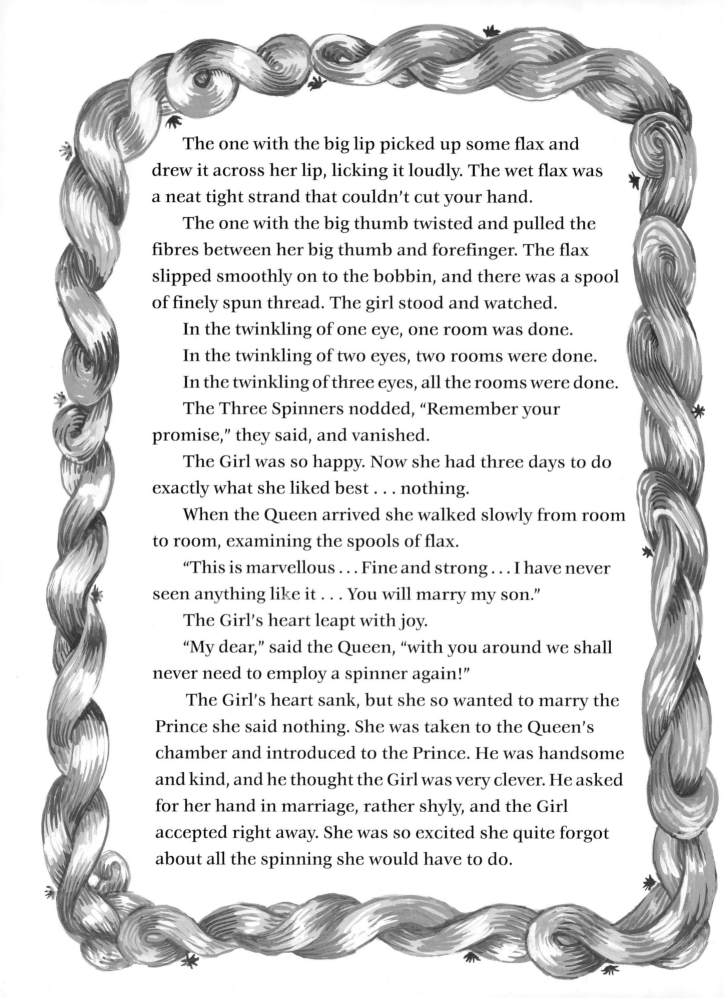

The one with the big lip picked up some flax and drew it across her lip, licking it loudly. The wet flax was a neat tight strand that couldn't cut your hand.

The one with the big thumb twisted and pulled the fibres between her big thumb and forefinger. The flax slipped smoothly on to the bobbin, and there was a spool of finely spun thread. The girl stood and watched.

In the twinkling of one eye, one room was done.

In the twinkling of two eyes, two rooms were done.

In the twinkling of three eyes, all the rooms were done.

The Three Spinners nodded, "Remember your promise," they said, and vanished.

The Girl was so happy. Now she had three days to do exactly what she liked best . . . nothing.

When the Queen arrived she walked slowly from room to room, examining the spools of flax.

"This is marvellous . . . Fine and strong . . . I have never seen anything like it . . . You will marry my son."

The Girl's heart leapt with joy.

"My dear," said the Queen, "with you around we shall never need to employ a spinner again!"

The Girl's heart sank, but she so wanted to marry the Prince she said nothing. She was taken to the Queen's chamber and introduced to the Prince. He was handsome and kind, and he thought the Girl was very clever. He asked for her hand in marriage, rather shyly, and the Girl accepted right away. She was so excited she quite forgot about all the spinning she would have to do.

They began to plan the wedding at once. The
invitations were sent out, and the Girl made sure she
invited her three aunts.

At last the day arrived, the rings were exchanged, the
promises made and the guests invited to a huge banquet.
Everyone in the kingdom was there to see the Prince and
his new bride. Everyone, except the three old ladies. The
Girl looked around and breathed a sigh of relief – perhaps
they were not going to come after all. Dinner was served
and the bride and groom sat at the high table, with all the
guests below them.

Then the doors burst open and in came the Three
Spinners. Everyone stared in silence, their forks raised to
their mouths. They all began to whisper at once.

"Goodness me, look at that foot."

"The lip, my dear, have you ever seen anything like it?"

"Who invited them?"

"That thumb is disgusting."

"Whose relations are they?"

The Girl was horrified. How could she call them her dearest aunts in front of such important guests? "If only the earth would open and swallow me up," she prayed, but of course it didn't. Her promise was not so easy to keep after all. But she summoned up all the courage and kindness she had inside her and walked across the room. All the guests stared as she said, "Welcome, my dearest aunts!" Then she bent and kissed each one, and a gasp went round the hall.

"Come and sit with us at the high table," she said. And she gave the Three Spinners the most important place, between her husband and herself.

The Prince welcomed them kindly, and turned to the one with the big foot.

"I am so glad you could come to our wedding," he said politely, then he didn't know what to say. All he could think about was her foot.

"Ummm . . . How did you get such a great big foot?"

"By treading, my son, by treading!" she replied.

"Oh," he said, and turned to the second old lady.

"I'm so glad you could come . . . How did you get such a great big lip?"

"By licking, my son, by licking."

"Oh, I see," he said thoughtfully, and turned to the third. "How did you get such a great big thumb?"

"By twisting, my son, by twisting."

"Oh, I *see*!" shouted the Prince. Suddenly he remembered all the spinning his wife had done. He leapt to his feet, raised his glass and proclaimed in a loud voice, "I would like it to be known that, from this day forth, my beautiful wife will never, ever, touch a spinning wheel again."

At that everybody cheered. But the bride's cheer was the loudest of all, because she never had, and she never would touch a spinning wheel again.

But perhaps she had done something far more difficult?

The three old ladies nodded.

Delgadina and

Once upon a time there was a little girl called Delgadina. She lived with her mother in a mountain village beside the sea. Everyone in the village scratched a living from the land by growing corn, keeping chickens and catching fish. They worked hard, but they were still poor.

One day Delgadina was walking in the mountains when she saw a tiny snake. The snake's skin was a brilliant emerald green.

"What a beautiful snake!" cried Delgadina. "I will look after him." And she picked up the snake and carried him home. She put the snake in a little clay pot and fed him crumbs of bread and drops of milk. Delgadina played with the snake every day, and fed him scraps of food. The snake began to grow, and as he grew, Delgadina grew up.

Soon the snake was too big for the pot, so Delgadina put him into an old wooden barrel. She fed him bread and milk and chunks of meat. And the snake grew and grew, and as he grew, Delgadina grew up.

Soon the snake was too big for the barrel, so Delgadina carried him to her bedroom, and put him into her cupboard. She fed the snake bread and milk and heaps of meat. And the snake grew and grew, and Delgadina

the Magic Snake

grew up, until she was sixteen years old.

One day Delgadina's mother said, "My dear, we are too poor to feed such a huge snake. You must let him go."

So Delgadina went to her bedroom and opened the cupboard door. The snake had grown so big he curled round and round inside the cupboard.

"My green snake," said Delgadina sadly, "we have given you all the food we have. We cannot look after you any more."

The green snake opened his mouth and spoke – in a human voice. "Delgadina," he hissed, "thank you for taking such good care of me. I want to give you something in return. Rub your hands over my eyes three times."

Delgadina put her hands on the snake's eyes. His skin was not wet, but smooth and dry. Delgadina rubbed her hands over the snake's eyes, once, twice, three times.

"Now," said the snake, "wash your hands, shake them dry, and you will see what you will see."

Then the snake slid out of the cupboard and through the cottage door. He slithered over the cliff and splashed into the ocean.

Delgadina ran and dipped her hands in the well. She

washed them carefully, then lifted them out of the water and began to shake them dry. As the drops of water fell from her fingertips they turned into golden coins. Delgadina shook and shook her fingers, and gold tumbled onto the ground. By the time her hands were dry, there was a huge pile of golden coins. She could hardly believe her eyes and rushed to show her mother.

"We will never be poor again," she laughed.

So Delgadina and her mother went to market and

bought fish and bread and fruit and wine, to celebrate.

Now, you might think it best to keep a gift of golden fingers to yourself. But not Delgadina. She was soon shaking piles of gold for all her friends and neighbours. News of her generosity spread throughout the land – until it reached the ears of the King.

When the King heard about the girl with the golden fingers and how kind she was, he liked her. And the more he heard about her, the more he liked her. He asked everyone who came to the palace if they knew Delgadina. He could think of nothing but Delgadina; he had fallen in love.

One day an old woman came to the palace. When the King asked her about Delgadina, she rubbed her hands together and a greedy look came into her eyes.

"Your Majesty," she said in a charming voice, "I know Delgadina, and I can arrange for her to marry you."

The King's heart swelled with happiness.

"All I will need," coaxed the old woman, "is a wedding dress and a golden coach with four white horses to bring her to the palace."

The King was so in love with Delgadina that, quick as a flash, he gave the old woman a wedding dress covered with diamonds, and a golden coach with four white horses.

"Bring Delgadina to me as soon as you can," he begged.

The old woman sat on top of the coach, cracked the whip and charged off. But not towards Delgadina's cottage. She drove until she came to her own house. For the old woman was really a witch.

"Come here, my daughter," she shrieked.

Out of the house came a girl, about sixteen years old, with a greedy look in her eyes.

"You are going to marry the King," said the Witch, opening the carriage door. "Get inside."

The Witch's Daughter climbed into the carriage, the witch cracked the whip, and they charged off.

They drove through the mountains and past the sea until they came to Delgadina's cottage. The golden coach pulled up outside and the Witch knocked on the door.

"The King wants to marry Delgadina," she gushed. "And here is the coach and wedding dress to prove it."

Delgadina gasped at the beautiful dress. She put it on and it fitted perfectly. She turned this way and that and the diamonds sparkled with light.

"Oh, it must be meant for me," she sighed. So Delgadina kissed her mother goodbye and climbed into the coach. The Witch cracked the whip and they charged off.

Then Delgadina saw there was another girl sitting in the corner of the carriage. The Witch's Daughter took out her handkerchief and pretended to cry.

"Oh, I wish I had a dress like that!" she sobbed. "It's not fair. I want a dress like that."

"Please don't cry," said Delgadina kindly. "I don't really need the dress, I can shake gold from my fingers any time. You can have it." Delgadina took the dress off. The Witch's Daughter put it on, and gave Delgadina her shabby old clothes instead.

"We must be nearly at the palace," smirked the Witch's Daughter. "Why don't you lean out of the window and wave to the King."

Delgadina stood up, opened the window and leant out of the carriage. They were not near the palace, but on top of a very high cliff. Suddenly, the Witch's Daughter pushed Delgadina, and the Witch pulled Delgadina. Together they hurled her out of the carriage and threw her over the cliff. Delgadina tumbled down the cliff to the rocks below.

"Ha, haa!" screamed the Witch. "Now, my daughter can marry the King." And she cracked the whip and they charged off.

When they arrived at the palace the King was waiting to greet Delgadina. He opened the carriage door and out stepped the Witch's Daughter.

"Welcome," said the King very politely, taking her by the hand.

"Show me the palace at once," demanded the Witch's Daughter.

The King thought this did not sound like Delgadina. "Surely you will need to wash your hands first?" he asked.

"What," cried the Witch's Daughter, "and waste the gold! I only wash my hands once a day, before breakfast."

The King thought this must be Delgadina after all. So that evening, he married her.

The next morning, before breakfast, a royal washbasin was brought for the Witch's Daughter. She dipped her hands into the water, lifted them out and shook them. The water dropped from her fingertips, fell upon the floor, and made a huge puddle!

"Look what you've done," snapped the Witch's Daughter. "I have lost all my magic by marrying you!"

The King knew at once that he had been tricked. This was not Delgadina. He had married the Witch's Daughter instead.

All this time Delgadina lay at the bottom of the cliff. Her body was broken and bruised, and two rocks had pierced her eyes. A fisherman found her and carried her to his hut. He took great care of her and gradually her bones mended and her bruises healed. But Delgadina's eyes would not heal. She was blind. So she learnt to use her fingers as her eyes. And every day she would feel her way down to the seashore and sit and listen to the waves.

One day Delgadina called out, "My green snake, if only you were with me now!"

Suddenly she heard a huge splash and there was the green snake. He had grown so much he filled the ocean.

"Delgadina," he hissed, "what is wrong?"

Delgadina told him the whole story.

"Rub your hands over my eyes, three times," hissed the snake.

Delgadina felt with her hands, and found the snake's eyes. Then she rubbed her hands over his eyes, once, twice three times.

"Now rub your hands over your own eyes, three times," hissed the snake.

So Delgadina rubbed her hands over her own eyes, once, twice, three times. When she took her hands away, she could see! Her eyes were completely healed, and they were a beautiful emerald green, just like the snake.

"Oh, thank you!" cried Delgadina.

"Climb on my back," said the snake. "I will take you home."

"There is something I must do first," replied Delgadina. And she ran to the fisherman's hut, dipped her hands into the well, and shook him a huge pile of gold. Then she climbed on to the snake's back and clung on tightly to his neck. The snake swam with her over the waves, until they reached her mother's cottage.

Delgadina ran up the path and peeped in through the window. Her mother was sitting at the kitchen table, weeping. Delgadina rushed in and threw her arms around her and kissed her. Then Delgadina went to the well, washed her hands and shook them a pile of gold. They went to market and bought fish and bread and fruit and wine, to celebrate.

Soon Delgadina was shaking piles of gold for all her friends and neighbours. The news spread throughout the land that Delgadina was back. And it reached the ears of the King! But he was married to the Witch's Daughter and, as you know, witches are very difficult to get rid of!

The King thought and thought and thought, until he had thought of a very good plan.

He said to the Witch's Daughter, "I want to give a party in your honour, and invite everyone in the land to marvel at your beauty."

The Witch's Daughter went wild with pride, and began her toilette at once. The King sent invitations to everyone, including Delgadina and her mother. A huge feast was prepared, the banqueting hall was decorated with flowers and the tables were laid with white cloths.

The guests arrived from all over the land, and among

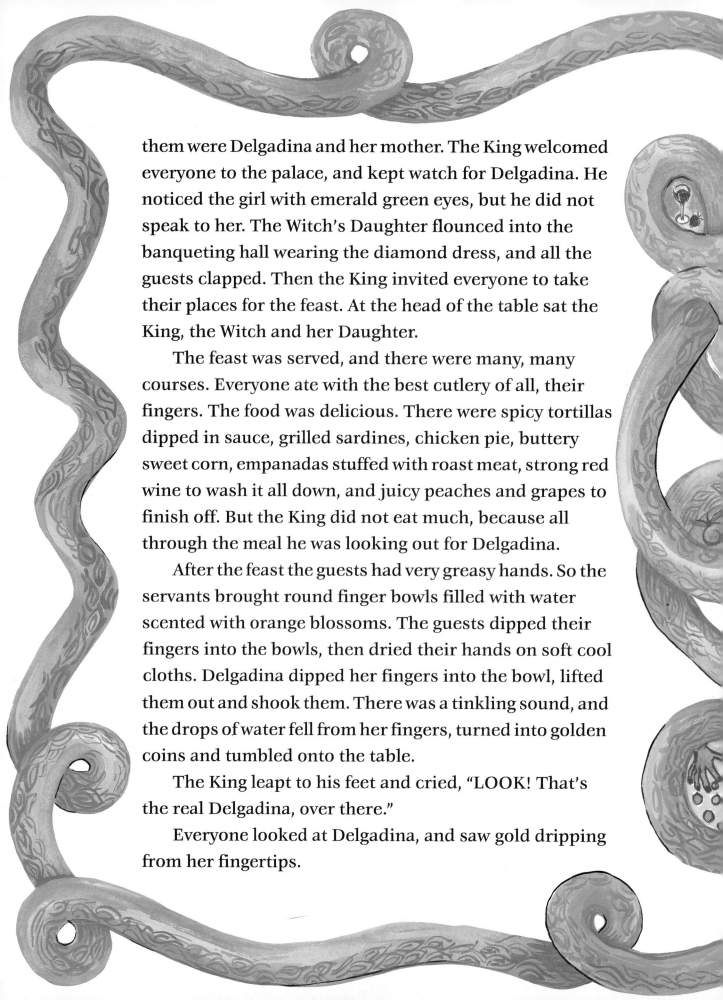

them were Delgadina and her mother. The King welcomed everyone to the palace, and kept watch for Delgadina. He noticed the girl with emerald green eyes, but he did not speak to her. The Witch's Daughter flounced into the banqueting hall wearing the diamond dress, and all the guests clapped. Then the King invited everyone to take their places for the feast. At the head of the table sat the King, the Witch and her Daughter.

The feast was served, and there were many, many courses. Everyone ate with the best cutlery of all, their fingers. The food was delicious. There were spicy tortillas dipped in sauce, grilled sardines, chicken pie, buttery sweet corn, empanadas stuffed with roast meat, strong red wine to wash it all down, and juicy peaches and grapes to finish off. But the King did not eat much, because all through the meal he was looking out for Delgadina.

After the feast the guests had very greasy hands. So the servants brought round finger bowls filled with water scented with orange blossoms. The guests dipped their fingers into the bowls, then dried their hands on soft cool cloths. Delgadina dipped her fingers into the bowl, lifted them out and shook them. There was a tinkling sound, and the drops of water fell from her fingers, turned into golden coins and tumbled onto the table.

The King leapt to his feet and cried, "LOOK! That's the real Delgadina, over there."

Everyone looked at Delgadina, and saw gold dripping from her fingertips.

The Witch's Daughter was terrified, and the Witch muttered, "We'd better get out of here, fast!"

They ran out of the hall and jumped into the golden carriage. The Witch cracked the whip and they charged off, out of the palace and along the cliff path. But the green snake heard them coming. He whipped his tail and it was so long and heavy it made a huge wave in the water. The wave swelled in the sea and crashed over the side of the cliff. It swept the Witch and her Daughter, the dress and the carriage, down, down, down, to the bottom of the sea. And they were never seen, or heard of, again!

But in the palace, all the guests rejoiced. At last they could celebrate the marriage of the real Delgadina to the King! And after the wedding the King and Delgadina went down to the sea to thank the great green snake.

They visited the snake for the rest of their lives, and their children visit him still.

The Sun

Iɴ the beginning, the Sky and the Earth had three children. Their eldest child was a daughter called Ama Terasu. She had fiery-red hair and was so beautiful that her parents had to shield their eyes to look at her.

"She is lovely," said her mother and father. "Everyone should see her!" And they put a golden necklace around her neck, and gave her a palace high up in the sky. Ama Terasu sat in the palace and her necklace shone so brightly it lit up the whole world. Ama Terasu became the Sun Goddess.

Their second child was a son called Suki. He had silver hair and was quiet and gentle. They gave him a palace in the night sky, and he became the Moon God.

Their youngest child was a son called Susa. He had blue-black hair that hung down to his knees, and a terrible temper. He raged and crashed about so much that he became the Storm God. He was not given a palace, but roamed the world, riding the dark storm clouds and howling around mountains.

Ama Terasu was the most powerful of the three. Her necklace warmed the world, and animals and people came into being. Her light made rice grow and humans happy.

Goddess

Everyone loved the Sun Goddess best of all.

Everyone except Susa. Whenever he saw the sun, he felt miserable. For his brother and sister both had splendid palaces, while he was homeless. He was doomed to dwell in cold treetops, and shelter on lonely hillsides. The nearest he got to a palace was to rattle its windows. So he decided to go and stay with his sister.

Susa strode towards heaven. The ground rumbled under his feet, mountains shook and rocks splashed into the sea. The noise echoed across earth, filled the air, and reached heaven.

"Susa must be coming to steal my necklace," thought Ama Terasu. "Well, he is not having it!"

So the Sun Goddess prepared for battle. She put her hair into two high warrior bunches. She dressed in a suit of armour, and slung her bow and quiver of arrows on her back. Then she went to the edge of heaven, where the Milky Way runs like a river. She stood on the Bridge of Heaven that crosses the Milky Way, and stamped her feet so firmly that her legs sank into the ground up to her thighs!

When Susa crashed to the other side of the bridge, he

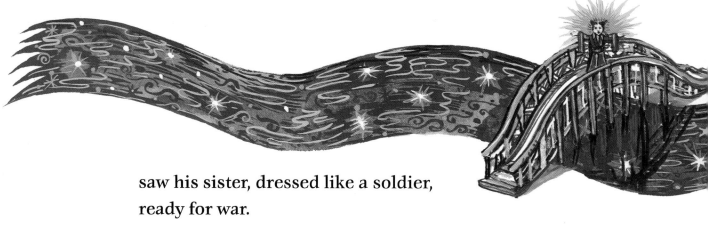

saw his sister, dressed like a soldier, ready for war.

"Sister, why are you armed against me?" he asked. "I have not come to fight."

"You want to steal my golden necklace," shouted Ama Terasu.

"Not at all!" bellowed her brother. "I am cold and lonely. All I want is to shelter in your palace."

"I don't believe you!" she cried. "If you haven't come to fight, give me your sword."

Susa pulled his sword from his belt and gave it to his sister.

"You won't be needing this any more," said Ama Terasu. And she put the sword over her knee, snapped it into three pieces, put the pieces in her mouth and chewed them up. Then she spat the mouthful into the Milky Way, and three new stars appeared.

"Now, you may be my guest!" she said, and welcomed Susa into her palace.

Susa had never seen anywhere so warm or clean. He wandered through golden halls and out into shining rice fields. As he walked he tossed his blue-black hair,

and there was a torrential rainstorm.
All the rice was flattened. Ama Terasu was very
cross with her brother and he promised to behave
himself. But the next day, as he walked through a
meadow, Susa stamped his foot and a wind blew down
all the fences. Although he promised not to destroy things,
he could not help himself, for he was the Storm God and it
was his nature. Just as the storm clouds cover up the sun,
so Susa upset his sister.

Then one day Ama Terasu was with her maidens in the
weaving hall. They were quietly weaving garments for the
large family of Gods, when suddenly there was a loud bang
and a chunk of ceiling crashed on to the floor. The maidens
screamed and Ama Terasu looked up to see her brother
peering through a huge hole in the roof! Susa roared with
laughter, then lowered a sturdy rope down through the
hole. Bound to the rope was a wild horse. The horse landed
at the Sun Goddess's feet, reared up and charged round
the hall. It smashed the looms, trampled the cloth,
and shuttles and bobbins flew everywhere. Then
Susa leapt through the hole himself, and swept
through the hall like a whirlwind, flooding
it with water.

"I'm not putting up with this any more," shouted Ama Terasu. "I'm going somewhere where you can't burst in."

And she ran out of the hall, over the fields and into the forest until she came to a cave. She ran inside the cave, and rolled a great rock across the entrance.

Suddenly the whole world was plunged into darkness. Heaven turned black and there was no light. During the night Suki the Moon did his best to light the world. But the sun did not rise. Day was as black as coal, the darkness a never-ending, eternal night. It was a terrible state of affairs. The rice would not grow, the animals were cold, and the people were afraid. All the ghosts and spirits who hid in dark corners freely roamed the earth.

The Gods went to the cave entrance and begged Ama Terasu to come out. The Sun Goddess listened to their request, but shook her head. "I am not coming out!" she cried.

The Gods tried to roll the rock aside, but it was too heavy. Only Ama Terasu could move it, and only Ama Terasu could restore order to the world. But how could they get her to come out of the cave? If they could not persuade her, perhaps they could trick her.

So the Gods went to the best blacksmith and asked him to forge a shining mirror. The blacksmith pumped up his fire and set to work. He melted rare metals and, tapping and pounding, forged a gleaming mirror. Then he polished the silvery surface until it shone.

The Gods and Goddesses carried the mirror to the cave. Beside the cave stood a graceful tree, and they hung the mirror on one of its branches. Then they decorated the tree with strings of sparkling jewels, and wove streamers of blue and white silk around the trunk. They hung lanterns to blow in the wind, and placed a white linen gown at the roots. They lit fires and burning torches, then summoned all the night birds to the cave entrance. These poor birds could not stop singing for day never dawned. So the singing birds of the eternal night sang and sang and sang. The nightingales trilled and the owls hooted.

Ama Terasu lay inside the cave and listened. "I am never coming out!" she shouted.

Then, Uzume, the Goddess of Dancing stepped forward. She picked a handful of withered bamboo leaves and arranged them into a fan. Everyone fell silent and watched. Uzume tilted her head, rolled her eyes and opened her fingers like the petals of a flower. She flicked her skirts and began to dance. She flew round in a circle, faster and faster and faster. The Gods clapped and Uzume stamped her feet furiously.

Ama Terasu listened. "I am not ever coming out!" she roared.

But Uzume did not stop dancing. She became a prowling lion, a leaping frog, a frisky pony. The Gods had never seen such a crazy dance. Then, suddenly, Uzume stood still, opened her eyes wide and fluttered her eyelashes, grinned and stuck out her tongue. The Gods cheered. Uzume raised her skirt, bent over, and wiggled her bottom! The Gods shrieked with laughter. They laughed until tears poured down their cheeks.

Inside the cave Ama Terasu listened. "What is so funny?" she fumed. "What are they doing out there?"

Ama Terasu just had to know. So she rolled the rock, just a tiny bit to one side, and peeped out. A beam of sunlight burst from the cave and fell upon Uzume. "How can you celebrate without me?" the Sun Goddess said stiffly.

"But, my lady," replied Uzume, "haven't you heard? We are celebrating because we have found someone who is more beautiful then you!"

"That's impossible," frowned Ama Terasu. "Who is it?"

"She is over there," said Uzume, pointing to the mirror. "Take a look at her yourself."

Ama Terasu looked at the mirror and could just see the face of someone so beautiful she had to shield her eyes. She came right out of the cave to look at her. And the world was flooded with light!

The Gods quickly stretched a rope, made of rice straw, across the entrance of the cave. Ama Terasu could not go back inside.

Ama Terasu went up to the mirror and stared into it. Her own reflection stared back.

"Oh!" she gasped. "Isn't she lovely! Who is she?"

"Sun Goddess," said Uzume gently, "who in the whole world could be more beautiful than you?"

And Uzume carefully dressed Ama Terasu in the white linen gown. "Please do not leave us again," she said. "We cannot live without you."

The Gods and Goddesses carried Ama Terasu back to

her palace. At last order had been restored to the world. The animals thrived, the rice waved in the wind, and the people were happy.

But Ama Terasu found Susa sulking in a corner.

"You need a palace of your own," she said kindly. "Where you can make as much noise, and as much mess as you like!" So she gave Susa a palace in the sea. And he has lived there ever since, crashing and splashing and pounding to his heart's content.

But once a year, during the winter, Susa visits his sister. He covers the sun with dark storm clouds and destroys the rice fields with floods. And just in case Ama Terasu hides in the cave, the people of Japan decorate a little tree with jewels and rice-straw ropes, to remind the Sun Goddess that they cannot live without her.

Master of all Masters

A YOUNG girl called Mollie wanted a job as a servant. So she went to the marketplace to try her luck, along with all the other boys and girls. One by one they were asked if they could cook and sew, mend shoes and chop wood. Then, if they were lucky, they were hired for a job of work. Mollie waited all day, but nobody hired her. She was just about to go home, when up came a coach drawn by four black horses. And out stepped a very large, richly dressed gentleman.

"Do you want a job, little girl?" he asked.

"Oh, yes please, sir," said Mollie.

"Then hop inside!" he said.

Mollie climbed into the coach and was taken up a hill to a huge mansion. Inside the house the important gentleman spoke, in a very important voice.

"Now, girl, if you want to work for me, there are some things you must learn. Everything in my house has its own special name. What, for instance, would you call me?"

"Oh, I would call you Sir, sir!"

"Wrong! You will call me MASTER OF ALL MASTERS!"

"Yes, Sir — oops — sorry, sir, I mean Master of all Masters, sir."

"Now what about this four-poster bed?"

"I would call it bed or couch."

"Wrong! You will call it my BARNACLE!"

Then he pointed at his smart black trousers. "What would you call these?"

"Trousers or... pants."

"Pants! Don't be so rude. These are my SQUIBBS AND CRACKERS."

Then he pointed at a small black and white cat. "What would you call this cat?"

"Cat or kit."

"No, she is WHITE-FACED SIMMINY."

Then he pointed at the grand fireplace. "And this?"

"Fireplace."

"Don't be so commonplace! You will call it HOT COCKALORUM. And what would you call this bucket of water?"

"Bucket or wet."

"You will call it PONDALORUM. Now, what about the whole house?"

"Castle or palace, Master of all Masters."

"Wrong! You will call it HIGH TOPPER MOUNTAIN."

Then he showed Mollie a little bedroom, and she soon fell fast asleep. But in the middle of the night she was woken by the smell of smoke and a strange crackling sound. Mollie leapt out of bed and rushed into the Master's bedroom. He was snoring loudly. She shook him and shouted:

"MASTER OF ALL MASTERS, get out of your BARNACLE and put on your SQUIBBS AND CRACKERS. WHITE-FACED SIMMINY has a spot of HOT COCKALORUM on her tail, and if you don't get some PONDALORUM, HIGH TOPPER MOUNTAIN will all be on HOT COCKALORUM!"

The message took so long to deliver, they just had time to run out of the front door before the whole house was burnt down to the ground.

Do you know what the message was?

The Golden Saucer

ONCE there was a poor peasant who lived with his daughter Katherine in a little cottage. They had a plot of land and kept a pig, a goat and a dove. The cottage had two rooms, one with a fire, where they cooked and ate and where the old man slept at night. The other was just big enough for Katherine's bed.

One day the Peasant was digging in the vegetable patch when his spade struck something hard. He brushed away the earth and there was a saucer, entirely made of gold.

"God has blessed us!" he shouted to his daughter. "This saucer must belong to the King. If I take it to him, he will give me a huge reward."

"Father, I wouldn't do that if I were you," said Katherine, shaking her head. "If you give the King the saucer, he will only want the cup."

"Don't be foolish, child. This is a golden saucer. The King will be delighted." And the Peasant put on his best old jacket, washed the saucer in the well, and set off across the fields for the palace.

He bowed low before the King and with great pride gave him the golden saucer. The King turned the saucer over and over in his hands.

"Thank you, very nice," he nodded. "WHERE IS THE CUP?" he bellowed.

"Your Majesty," replied the Peasant nervously. "I didn't find a cup."

"No cup? What do you mean, man? Wherever there is a saucer, there is always a cup. My kitchen is full of them!"

The old man began to tremble. "I am sorry . . ."

"This man is a thief and a liar," shouted the King. "Throw him in the dungeon at once."

Two large guards marched the Peasant down to the dungeon. It was cold and dark. There was nothing to eat but dry bread and water, and nothing to lie on but cobwebs and rats' droppings. The old man put his head in his hands and began to cry. "If only I had listened to my daughter." Big tears splashed on to the dungeon floor. "If only I had listened to my daughter." He cried all day. "If only I had listened to my daughter." He cried all night. "If only, if only, if only . . .!" His cries got louder and louder. And echoed all over the palace . . . and into the King's bedroom!

"Aaaahhhh!" cried the King. "I haven't slept a wink with that man's hullabaloo. Bring him to me at once."

The Peasant was brought before the King.

"Not only have you stolen the King's gold," fumed the King, "you have kept him awake all night by crying. What are you going on about?"

"Well, Your Majesty," replied the Peasant, "my daughter told me not to give you the saucer because you would only want the cup. So you see, if only I had listened to my daughter, I wouldn't be here now."

"She is one of those girls is she?" said the King. "Let's see if she's really so clever." And the King handed the Peasant a single stalk of flax. "My army needs new shirts," he said. "Tell your daughter to make the shirts for me from this flax. By tomorrow morning."

"But…" stuttered the old man.

"Dismissed!" cried the King.

So the Peasant set off across the fields for home.

"Oh dear, what am I going to do?" he mumbled. "I might as well be in the dungeon. This flax must be stripped and beaten, washed and dried, spun into thread, woven into cloth and stitched into shirts. By tomorrow. And there isn't even enough flax to sew on a button! Oh, why didn't I listen to my…"

"Father," cried Katherine, "where have you been?" She listened to his story, and did not say, "I told you so." She bent down to the hearth and picked up a chip of wood from among the ashes. "If I were you, this is what I would do. Go to the King and tell him…" and she whispered into her father's ear.

So the old man set off for the palace, and bowed before
the King.

"Your Majesty, my daughter would be honoured to
make shirts for all your soldiers, but she hasn't got a loom.
She says, could you please make her one, from this piece of
wood. By tomorrow." And he gave the King the tiny chip of
wood. The King turned the wood chip in his fingers and the
Peasant began to tremble.

"I'd like to meet this daughter of yours," said the King.
"Tell her to come and see me,

Not clothed, but not naked
Not walking, but not riding
Not on the road, but not off the road
Bringing a gift, that is not a gift!"

"But . . ." pleaded the Peasant.

"Dismissed!" cried the King.

The Peasant set off across the fields. "Dear, oh dear," he
moaned. "We might as well chop our own heads off. If only
I had…"

Katherine listened to the whole story. "Fetch me the old fishing net," she said, and began taking off her clothes.

"Where is this going to end?" groaned the old man.

Katherine wrapped herself up in the fishing net. She wasn't clothed, but then she wasn't naked.

She took the goat by the horns and straddled it. She wasn't walking, but then she wasn't riding.

She stood on the road and put her big toe in the muddy ditch at the side of the road. She wasn't on the road, but then she wasn't off the road.

Then, catching the dove up under one arm, she set off for the palace.

The King looked out of his topmost window, and what a sight met his eyes. He began to giggle, he began to splutter. He held his sides and roared with laughter.

"Not clothed, but not naked — very good. Not walking, but not riding — clever. Not on the road, but not off the road — brilliant. Where's the gift?" And he charged down the spiral staircase and through the palace gates.

"Where's the gift, that is not a gift?" he demanded.

"Your Majesty," smiled Katherine. "Please accept this . . ." She held the dove out to the King and opened her hands.

"Crrroooo . . ." The dove flew away!

The King beamed. "Excellent! You may marry me and be my wife. There is only one condition, I am the King and my word is final. Whatever I say, goes."

So there was a huge wedding. Everybody was invited, and everybody was delighted to have such a kind-hearted girl as their Queen. The wedding lasted for seven days and seven nights. The inns were packed with people feasting from dawn to dusk. Drinking and dancing, singing and storytelling, and sleeping in between!

One stable was crammed full with carts and horses. On the seventh night a farmer's mare gave birth to a baby foal. The next morning a merchant found the foal curled up underneath his cart. When the merchant saw this he hatched a crafty plan.

"Oh my!" he cried. "A miracle has taken place during the night. My cart has given birth to a baby foal!"

Everybody crowded round to get a closer look, including the farmer.

"Excuse me," the farmer said angrily. "That foal belongs to me. My mare gave birth to it."

"But I found it underneath my cart," replied the merchant. "It now belongs to me."

The farmer and the merchant argued, then shouted, and then they began to fight. In the end they decided to take the matter to the King.

They stood before the throne, while the farmer told his story and the merchant told his. The King and Katherine listened.

"When I was a boy," pondered the King, "we always used to say finders keepers. So finders keepers it is. The foal belongs to the merchant. Dismissed!"

Katherine's mouth fell open. How could the King be so unfair? But she was not allowed to say anything. So she ran after the farmer.

"My good man," she whispered, "if I were you, this is what I would do . . ." And she handed him the old fishing net.

The next day, when the King was out hunting, he saw the farmer fishing in a pile of dust! The farmer was casting out the fishing net and hauling it in, pretending it was full of fish.

The King pulled up his horse and roared with laughter. "Have you gone quite mad, man?" he cried. "You will never catch fish in a pile of dust, not in a hundred years."

"But, Your Majesty," replied the farmer, "didn't you know? It is as easy to catch fish on dry land as it is for a cart to give birth to a foal!"

The King froze and his face turned the colour of

beetroot. "Very well," he boomed, "the foal is yours, but those words are not. Someone put you up to this, and I know just who it is."

The King wheeled his horse round, charged back to the palace and called for Katherine. "I told you, my word is final!" he shouted. "Whatever I say, goes. You have disobeyed me, and this marriage is over. You are dismissed!"

Katherine went quite pale, and the King softened a little. "But you may eat supper here first," he said. "And take one thing with you when you go, whatever it is that is dearest and best in your eyes."

So supper was served, but it was not a jolly affair. Katherine ate in silence and the King drank rather a lot of wine. Then Katherine secretly poured a sleeping potion into his sweet dessert wine. The King drank down the wine and fell asleep with his face in his pudding!

Katherine called the servants, and they carefully undressed the King, down to his kingly boxer shorts. They wrapped him in a linen sheet, put him in the royal carriage and set off for Katherine's cottage. Katherine put the King in her own bedroom, and she slept by the fire with her father.

The King slept all that night and all the next day. In the middle of the next night he awoke with a start. The bed was dreadfully hard. The sheets were all scratchy. Then he sat

up and banged his head on the ceiling.

"Servant!" he called. He heard a grunting sound, and the pig came in! "Help, help!" he shouted. "Where am I?"

Katherine awoke, lit a candle, and sat on the end of the King's bed. "You are at home with me, my lord," she said kindly. "You said that I could take one thing with me when I left, whatever it was that was dearest and best in my eyes. So I have taken you."

The King suddenly felt very ashamed. Big tears rolled down his cheeks. "You can't still love me after all I have done?"

"Of course I do," Katherine replied. "As you said in your own words, finders keepers."

So they decided to get married all over again. And this time it was a real wedding. It was even bigger than the first, and lasted fourteen days and fourteen nights. And all the army had new shirts – I don't know who made them!

But from that day onwards, whenever the King sat in judgement, he would turn to Katherine and say, "What do you think, my dear?"

Anansi's Daughter

A NANSI is half man, half spider, but one hundred per cent greedy. He can change his shape whenever he wants, but he is always getting into trouble.

One summer it was very hot. The sun burnt like a giant furnace. There wasn't a cloud in the sky and it hadn't rained for months. The streams dried up, the crops withered, and there was nothing left to eat. Nothing in Mrs Anansi's cupboards, nothing in the garden, and nothing in the fields. So Anansi sent his children to look for food.

Anansi's eldest daughter went into the forest. It was cool and shady. She looked on bushes for fruit and under stones for roots. But she didn't find anything. Then she saw a nut tree. But when she got closer, the tree only had three nuts. "Three nuts will not feed my family," she sighed. "But if I eat the nuts myself, at least I will have more strength to look for food."

So Anansi's Daughter picked the nuts, and found a stone to crack the shells. She crouched on the ground, and brought the stone down — *crack* — on the first nut. It bounced down a large hole. "Oh, bother!" she said.

She brought the stone down — *crack* — on the second nut, and that bounced down the hole. "Oh bother!" she cried. "If this last nut jumps down that hole, I'll jump down there myself and get it back!" And — *crack* — the third nut flew down the hole!

At that, Anansi's Daughter peered into the hole. It was

so dark she couldn't see the bottom. But she took a deep breath and jumped. It was a long way down. A very long way down. She fell through a starry sky, she fell past the moon, past leaves and through branches. She tumbled into a sunny day, and landed on a soft mossy bank. Anansi's Daughter had fallen into the underworld.

She rubbed her eyes, and saw a lush green field and a little hut. Beside the hut sat a wrinkled old woman cracking nuts with her teeth.

"Mmmm hmmm, delicious!" said the old woman.

Anansi's Daughter thought that the nuts looked just like the ones she'd lost. But she said nothing.

"Are you hungry?" asked the old woman.

Anansi's Daughter nodded.

"Well, there are lots of sweet potatoes growing in the field," the old woman replied. "The big potatoes will be calling '*Eat me!*' and the little potatoes will be calling '*Don't eat me!*' Take this spade, dig up the little potatoes and bring them to me."

Anansi's Daughter took the spade, and went into the field. She saw huge, juicy potatoes calling out *"Eat me, eat me!"* She was starving and they looked tasty. Then she saw tiny, shrivelled potatoes calling out *"Don't eat me, don't eat me!"* They did not look tasty at all. But she remembered what the old woman had said, and dug the little potatoes up.

"Now, child," said the old woman. "Peel the potatoes. Put the peel in the pot, and throw away the insides."

Anansi's Daughter had never heard of a recipe like that before. But she peeled the potatoes, threw away the wizened insides, and put the muddy peel into the pot. The pot began to bubble. Then Anansi's Daughter poured the peelings into two bowls, and they sat down to eat.

The old woman picked up her spoon and ate, but not with her mouth. She began eating through her nose, and eating through her ears! Anansi's Daughter had never seen eating like that before. But she was very polite, and said nothing. She picked up her spoon, and wondered what muddy potato peelings would taste like.

"Mmmm hmmm, delicious!" she cried

They were the tastiest thing she had ever eaten.

"Thank you, child," said the old woman. "I would like to give you something in return." She showed Anansi's Daughter a door at the back of the hut. "Go inside, and choose the smallest drum."

Anansi's Daughter opened the door. Inside was a room full of drums. Drums of every size and shape. Huge drums decorated with carvings, medium-sized drums with curved sticks and coloured skins, and little drums covered in

beads and tinkling bells. Then she saw the smallest drum. It was old, and worn, and plain. Anansi's Daughter badly wanted one of the big, beautiful drums, but she remembered what the old woman had said, and chose the smallest plainest drum.

"Take the drum home, play it, and shout *COVER!*" advised the old woman. Then she showed Anansi's Daughter a path that led into the forest. Anansi's Daughter thanked the old woman, and set off with the little drum under her arm.

She had hardly taken a few steps along the path, when she found herself back in our world. There were her father, Anansi, her mother and brothers and sisters.

"What have you got?" they cried.

She showed them her drum

"A drum!" sneered Anansi. "What good is that? We're hungry, we want food, not music."

But Anansi's Daughter sat on the ground and began to play the drum.

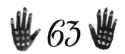

Ta te, ta te te, ta ta taa.

Faster and faster and faster.

Ta te, ta te te, ta ta TAA!

"COVER!" she cried.

Suddenly the whole floor was covered with food. There was rice and peas, fried saltfish and dumplings, spicy patties and plantain, fresh pineapple and cool sarsaparilla juice to wash it all down. Everyone was amazed. But not for long! They fell on the food and feasted until there wasn't a crumb left. Then they all lay down to doze in the sun.

Everyone, except Anansi. Because Anansi was thinking to himself, "Where did she get such a wonderful drum?"

The next day Anansi's Daughter told her father the whole story. All about the nuts, and the hole and . . . But before she had time to finish, Anansi had run off into the forest.

He found the tree, and sure enough, there were only three nuts on it. He picked them, took a stone and brought it down — *crack* — on the first nut. It did not jump down the hole. The shell cracked, and out popped a juicy nut. Anansi ate it.

"Mmmm hmmm, delicious!"

He brought the stone down — *crack* — on the second nut, and ate that. Then — *crack* — and the third nut was in

his mouth. He picked up all the shells and threw them down the hole, then peered into the darkness. "I am not jumping down there," he grumbled.

So he turned himself into a spider and spun a web, then lowered himself down the hole on a long silken thread. Anansi the spider swung through the starry sky, past the moon, past leaves and through branches. He dropped into a sunny day, landed on the mossy bank, and turned himself back into a man.

There sat the wrinkled old woman with a pile of empty shells in her lap.

"Mmmm hmmm," she said. "Are you hungry?"

"Yes," said Anansi, brushing the crumbs from his mouth.

"Well, there are lots of sweet potatoes growing in the field," said the old woman. "The big potatoes are calling '*Eat me!*' and the little potatoes are calling '*Don't eat me!*' Dig up the little potatoes and bring them to me."

Anansi took the spade and went into the field. The huge, juicy potatoes were calling "*Eat me, eat me!*" The tiny shrivelled potatoes were calling "*Don't eat me! Don't eat me!*"

"I am not eating those dried-up things!" he complained. So Anansi dug the big potatoes up.

"Now peel the potatoes," said the old woman. "Put the peel in the pot and throw away the insides."

Anansi had never heard anything so ridiculous. But he peeled the potatoes. The peel was covered in grit and mud.

"Ugghh," he shivered, "I can't possibly eat that!" So he

put the juicy insides into the pot, and threw away the peel. The pot began to bubble. Anansi served up the potatoes, making sure he had the biggest helping. Then they sat down to eat.

The old woman picked up her spoon, and began eating through her nose, and eating through her ears.

"How disgusting!" cried Anansi. "Have you no manners at all? You should eat like me."

He picked up his spoon. "Yuck!" he spluttered. "That tastes revolting." He pushed his bowl away — it was the worst thing he had ever eaten.

"Thank you," said the old woman. "I would like to give you something in return."

She showed him the door at the back of the hut. "Go inside, choose the smallest drum, take it home, play it and shout COVER!" she advised.

Anansi opened the door. He stared at the biggest drum and thought, "If the little drum gives food, what will the big drum give?"

He snatched up the biggest drum and raced back to the hole. The old woman didn't even have time to show him the path out of the underworld.

"He hey!" laughed Anansi. "This drum will give me ten times more food, and probably gold as well!"

He turned himself back into a spider, spun a web and wove a thread around the drum. Then he began to pull himself, and the drum, out of the hole. The drum was heavy and it was a long way up.

A very long way up. Panting and groaning Anansi pulled the drum through branches, past leaves, past the moon, through the starry sky and back into our world. Then he turned himself into a man, and carried the drum home.

When he arrived everyone was asleep. "Good!" he whispered. "I won't have to share my drum with anyone."

He sat down and, very quietly, he began to play.

Ta te, ta te te, ta ta taa.

Faster and faster and faster.

Ta te, ta te te, ta ta TAA!

"COVER!" he cried.

Suddenly Anansi was covered in spots. Covered in huge red and yellow and green spots!

"*Ahhhhhh!*" he screamed.

He was covered in spots from head to toe!

"*Help!*" he shouted.

Everyone woke up and rushed outside to see what the matter was. Anansi was rolling on the ground, covered in

spots. His children began to laugh. Mrs Anansi shook her head and said, "Oh dear, you must be very ill, Anansi. Very ill indeed. You must go to bed right now and stay there until all the spots have gone. And with spots that colour, you better not eat anything."

So Anansi lay in bed for a whole week. He listened to his daughter playing her drum and shouting "COVER!", and everyone feasting and having a good time. Everyone except Anansi. Because he wasn't even allowed a crumb.

After that, Anansi never went near the drum, or down to the underworld, ever again.

Mmmm hmmm!
Anansi made his fun.
And me, I want none.

Sedna under

Long, long ago, when the world had just been made and humans understood the language of animals, there were no fish or creatures in the sea.

A young woman called Sedna lived with her five brothers in the vast icy wastelands of the Arctic. During the summer months they lived in a tent and hunted caribou and fox. When winter came they built an igloo from blocks of snow, and huddled inside eating dried meat from their store. When the meat ran out, they went hungry.

Sedna was very beautiful. She had long black plaits, rosy cheeks and shining black eyes. Many young men wanted to marry her, but Sedna was proud and she turned them all down.

Now Raven was King of the Birds, and he wanted a wife and his beady eyes fell upon Sedna. "She won't marry a human," he croaked, "but she will marry me!"

Raven fluttered his wings, muttered a spell, stamped his claws and danced around in a circle. His beak and feathers disappeared, and there stood a handsome man with raven-black hair. He put on a pair of reindeerskin

the Sea ✦

boots and a parka of white wolverine fur. Then he looked at his reflection in the sea. "Very tasty," he preened, "except for the eyes." They still looked like birds' eyes. So he found a little bone and carved a pair of snow goggles, with a tiny slit for each eye to peer out of. "Now she will never know," he squawked. Then he climbed into his canoe and paddled across the bay.

Sedna was cutting up meat with her silver crescent-shaped knife. She heard the splash of the paddle in the water, but carried on working. Raven got out of the canoe and stood on the edge of the shore. He put one hand on his hip and tapped the ground with his foot. He gave a long, slow whistle. Sedna looked up and saw a splendid man in fine reindeerskin boots and a wolverine parka.

"Hello there," Raven crooned. "I'm the King!" He ruffled his hair. "Are you in love with me yet?"

Sedna put down her knife and got up. She did not say hello to Raven, or goodbye to her brothers. She just climbed into the canoe and Raven paddled away.

Raven charmed her, and flattered her. Raven paddled

across the bay and by the time he reached the other side, Sedna was in love. She was so in love, she didn't notice Raven unfurl two black wings, lift her high in the air and drop her into a nest. She was so in love, she thought the nest was a castle with many rooms, she didn't even feel the wind or the salt-stinging spray of the sea. She was so in love, she thought the raw meat Raven gave her to eat was roasted.

This went on – until one very windy day. A gust of wind blew so hard that it blew Raven's goggles right off. Sedna saw his beady bird's eyes. Suddenly the spell was broken and Sedna's eyes were opened. She saw that she was sitting in a nest at the top of a cliff, and that her husband had claws, wings and a beak! "Help!" she cried. "I married a bird. Help, Brothers, I married a bird!"

"Caw!" called Raven, and flew off to fetch some food to stop her crying.

Sedna shouted louder and louder, and her cries carried across the water. Her brothers heard her and jumped into a boat. They paddled across the bay, following their sister's cries, till they saw Sedna perched in a nest at the top of a cliff.

"I married a bird!" she sobbed.

Her eldest brother scrambled up the cliff, lifted Sedna into his arms and helped her down into the boat. "We must get away from here quickly," he urged. "If Raven returns, we will all be dead."

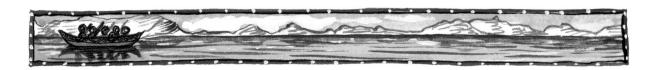

The brothers paddled as fast as they could, speeding through the sea. Suddenly a dark shadow fell upon the boat and they heard the whirring of wings. Raven had returned and he saw his wife being stolen away. "Caw! caw!" he croaked. "Give me back my bride!"

Raven began to beat his wings faster and faster and faster. He beat the wind into a storm. The wind wailed and whistled. He whipped the sea up into a foam, until waves crashed against the side of the boat.

The brothers were terrified. "We must give Sedna back to Raven," they cried, "or we'll all be killed in this storm!"

The wind howled and waves lashed the boat. "Here bird, take her!" shouted the brothers. And they threw Sedna over the side of the boat, into the sea.

Sedna sank down under the waves. She could see the bottom of the boat, and swam up and clung on to the side

with her hands. But her brothers were afraid. They did not want to die. So they lifted their paddles out of the sea, and brought them down — SMACK — on to Sedna's five fingers. Her hands were so cold, that her fingertips snapped off like icicles, and tumbled into the sea. As they touched the water, the fingertips turned into fishes and swam away.

Sedna sank down into the icy green water. Then up she rose and clung on to the side of the boat with her knuckles. Her brothers brought their paddles down — SMACK. Her knuckles snapped off, tumbled into the sea, and turned into seals and swam away.

Sedna sank down, then up she rose and clung on to the side of the boat with the stumps of her fingers. Her brothers brought the paddles down — SMACK. The stumps snapped off, tumbled into the sea, and turned into walrus and swam away.

Sedna sank down, then up she rose and clung on to the side of the boat with her thumbs. Her brothers brought the paddles down — SMACK. Her thumbs snapped off, tumbled into the sea, and turned into two great whales and swam away.

Sedna had no fingers left. She could no longer cling on to the boat, and sank down under the waves. Raven had lost his bride for ever. He stopped flapping his wings, and the storm vanished. The brothers were safe at last, but they had lost their sister, and they paddled home alone.

Sedna sank down and down and down, to the bottom of the sea. But the seals and whales caught her, and carried her to an underwater cave. And there they made a house for her. Sedna became the Mother of the Sea, cared for by all the children who had been born from her fingers. From that day onwards, the sea was full of creatures.

Sedna did not forget about her brothers, and she sent them some fish to eat. Soon everyone on land was learning how to catch fish through holes in the ice, and how to make nets and harpoons. Now, even during the hard winter months, the people never went hungry.

The Mother of the Sea basked in her cave, and her hair grew longer and longer and longer, until it was tangled with shells and seaweed, and knotted with barnacles and fishing nets. Sedna's hair was terribly uncomfortable; the shells scratched and the nets pulled. But Sedna could not comb out the tangles or plait her hair because she did not have any fingers. She was so irritated that she thrashed around at the bottom of the sea, and huge waves splashed on the shore. The sea was very rough, no one could go fishing, their nets were torn to shreds and they couldn't catch anything. Soon, the people were hungry again.

In the end, Sedna's eldest brother said, "Something is the matter with Sedna. I will go down to the bottom of the ocean and see if she is all right."

He took a canoe and paddled far out to the centre of the sea. A whirlpool came and carried him down under the

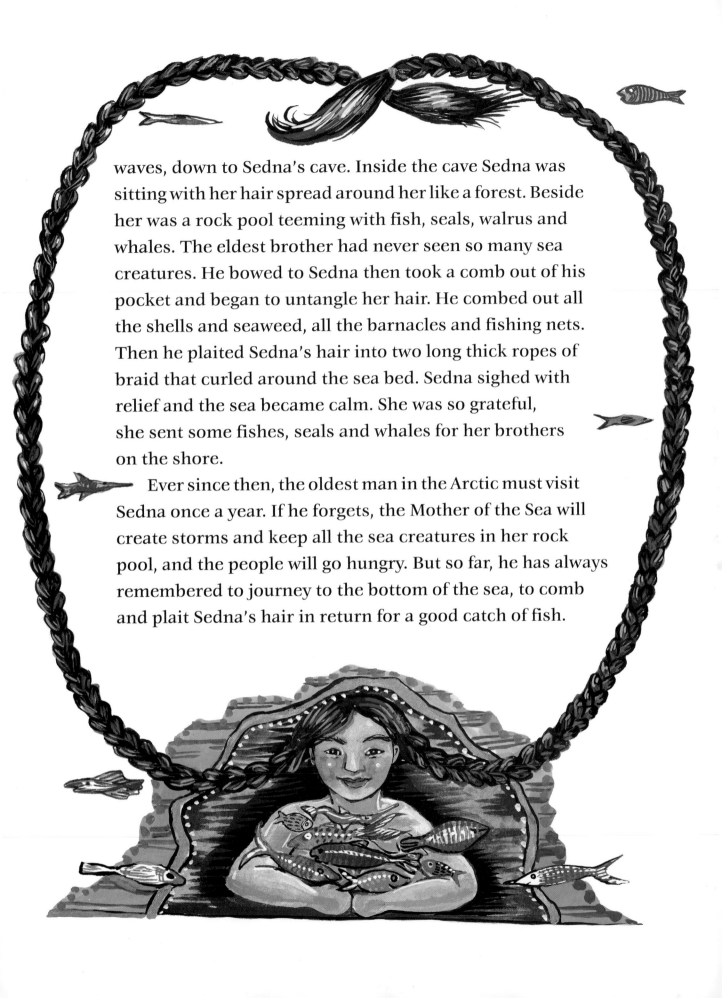

waves, down to Sedna's cave. Inside the cave Sedna was sitting with her hair spread around her like a forest. Beside her was a rock pool teeming with fish, seals, walrus and whales. The eldest brother had never seen so many sea creatures. He bowed to Sedna then took a comb out of his pocket and began to untangle her hair. He combed out all the shells and seaweed, all the barnacles and fishing nets. Then he plaited Sedna's hair into two long thick ropes of braid that curled around the sea bed. Sedna sighed with relief and the sea became calm. She was so grateful, she sent some fishes, seals and whales for her brothers on the shore.

Ever since then, the oldest man in the Arctic must visit Sedna once a year. If he forgets, the Mother of the Sea will create storms and keep all the sea creatures in her rock pool, and the people will go hungry. But so far, he has always remembered to journey to the bottom of the sea, to comb and plait Sedna's hair in return for a good catch of fish.

The Clever Cook

ONCE there was a cook called Gretel. She worked for a rich man, and lived in the attic at the top of his house. Gretel had the most beautiful pair of red shoes. Every morning she would put on her shoes, stand in front of the mirror, turn this way and that, click her heels together, and say, "Gretel, you are the cleverest cook in the land!" Then she would set about her day's work, for she was an excellent cook, and loved good food and good wine.

As soon as her Master was out, Gretel would sneak down to the cellar and pour herself a glass of wine. "Here's to you, Gretel!" she would say, raising the glass and gulping down the wine. This made her very hungry. So she would go back to the kitchen and cook herself the best bacon and eggs, taking care to wipe the grease from both corners of her mouth so that her master would be none the wiser.

One day her Master came into the kitchen. "A Very Important Guest is coming for supper tonight," he announced. "I want to impress him. Roast two chickens, and make sure they are cooked perfectly. If they are even the tiniest bit burnt, Gretel, you are out."

So Gretel put on her apron and went into the yard. She caught two chickens. She chopped off their heads, and chopped off their tails. She pulled out their insides, and plucked out their feathers. She basted them well, then put them on the spit over the fire, and turned the spit round and round.

Soon the meat began to cook. The juices sizzled on to the coals below, and the skin began to crisp and crinkle. The chickens smelt delicious. Gretel called to her Master, "Sir, the chickens are nearly cooked."

"Good, good!" said her Master, rubbing his hands. "I will go and fetch the guest." And he put on his hat and coat and went out into the windy night.

Gretel sat by the fire and turned the spit. It was hot and thirsty work. So she sneaked down to the cellar and poured herself a large glass of wine. "Here's to you, Gretel!" she said, gulping it down. This made her very hungry.

She went back to the kitchen and looked at the chickens. "Oh dear!" she said. "One of the wings is a tiny bit burnt. My Master will not be pleased." And quick as a flash, she pulled the burnt wing off. Now he would be none the wiser!

She looked at the crispy, brown wing. "It would be a shame to waste it," she thought. So she tasted it, and it was delicious.

"Oh dear!" she said. "Now the chicken has one wing on, and one wing off. That will never do. I'd better pull the other wing off to even it up." And off came the second wing, and it would be a shame to waste it, so she ate it.

"Oh dear!" she said. "Now one chicken has wings, and one chicken has none. I'd better pull off the other wings, then he won't notice the difference." And off came the other two wings, and it would be a shame to waste them, so down they went, the same way.

Then Gretel ran to the window and looked out. There was no sign of her Master or the Guest. All she could see was lashing rain.

"Perhaps they are waiting until the rain stops?" she thought. "It would be a shame to waste the chickens. Someone should eat them. And the only someone here . is me!"

So Gretel pulled one chicken off the spit then sat down at the kitchen table and gobbled it up. She smacked her lips, and looked longingly at the other chicken.

"Oh dear!" she said. "Now you're lonely. You chickens hatched together, scratched in the yard together, were roasted together, and now you're apart. Gretel," she said to herself, "be kind and send that chicken down to its friend."

And that is just what she did. Gretel pulled the second chicken off the spit, and soon there was a huge pile of bones on her plate. She was just wiping the grease from both corners of her mouth, when she heard the front door open. It was the Master.

"The Guest is on his way, Gretel," he called out. "The chickens smell excellent. I am just going to open a bottle of wine, and sharpen the carving knife."

The Master went into the dining room. He opened the wine, and picked up the sharpening stone. He began to swipe the blade of the carving knife back and forth across the stone. SHHHT… SHHHT… SHHHT!

Then there was a polite tap at the front door. Gretel smoothed her apron and went to answer the door. There stood a large man.

"I am the Very Important Guest," he said. "I have come to supper."

"Uhh…" said Gretel, thinking very fast. "Can you hear that noise?"

The Guest listened and heard, SHHHT… SHHHT… SHHHT, coming from the dining room. "It sounds like someone sharpening the carving knife," said the Guest. "It must be meat we are having for supper." And he patted his Very Important Stomach.

"Yes, it is meat," said Gretel quickly, "and the meat is going to be you!"

"Don't be ridiculous," laughed the Guest.

"But sir, my Master is a very evil man," whispered Gretel urgently. "He invites people to dinner, then ties them to a chair. He cuts off both their ears, roasts them on a spit, and serves the ears up on toast! Please sir, run away from here, as fast as you can."

SHHHT… SHHHT… SHHHT! The knife sounded very sharp indeed, and the Guest turned on his heels and ran.

Then Gretel flew into the dining room, raised her hands in the air, and cried, "Oh, Master, your Very Important Guest has just come into the kitchen, taken the chickens, and run off with them!"

"What!" shouted the Master. "But I'm starving. Didn't he even leave one chicken?"

"No sir," said Gretel, "he took them both."

"Greedy fellow," snorted the Master. "I'm going to get one back."

With that the Master ran out of the house, waving the carving knife in the air and calling, "Come back here, you scoundrel! That's my supper you're running away with!

Just let me have one, you can keep the other one. Please…
just one!"

The poor Guest thought he meant just one ear. He
clapped his hands over his ears and ran even faster. The
Guest ran and the Master ran, until the Guest came to his
own front door. He rushed inside and bolted the door tight.
He sighed with relief: he still had both his ears! The Master
went home wet and bedraggled, and very hungry.

But as for Gretel, she looked in her mirror, turned this
way and that, clicked her red heels together and said,
"Gretel, what a clever cook you are."

For she was full, and she was merry, and no one was any
the wiser. Except for you!

The White

ONCE upon a time, in the snowy mountains of the north, lived a King and a Queen who had three daughters. The King loved his daughters dearly, but his youngest daughter was so sweet and pretty, he loved her best of all.

One night, the youngest Princess dreamt of a golden ring entwined with flowers. The ring was so beautiful that when the Princess awoke she set her heart on having it.

"Of course you shall have the ring," said her father.

And a ring was made, just like the one in her dream. But when the Princess put it on, it was too big. Another was made and it was too small. The Princess began to feel ill. "If I don't have that ring," she declared, "I will die."

The doctor was called, and he advised nourishing soup and plenty of fresh air. Every day the Princess sipped some soup and took a walk. But all she thought about was the ring.

Then one day, as the Princess walked through the forest, she saw a huge white bear. He had a crown on his head, and between his paws he held the golden ring.

"That's my ring!" cried the Princess.

"No, it's mine," growled the Bear.

"How much do you want for it?" she asked.

"A ring such as this," replied the Bear, "is not to be had for money."

"What *do* you want then?" she demanded.

Bear King

"To marry you."

"Marry a bear!" laughed the Princess. But she wanted the ring so badly, she said, "Very well, I will marry you."

The Bear put the ring on her finger, and it fitted perfectly. "I'll come for you on Thursday," he said.

The Princess ran back to the castle. "Father," she cried happily, "I have my ring!" And she told him the whole story.

"Marry a bear?" shouted the King. "Certainly not!" And he ordered his soldiers on to the castle battlements, with bows and arrows ready.

When Thursday came, the Bear lumbered over the drawbridge, and hundreds of arrows whistled through the air. But the arrows bounced off the Bear's back, and he bounded into the castle unharmed. He found the King sitting on his throne, and the three Princesses hiding behind it. "I've come for my bride," he growled.

The King thought fast. "A bear won't know the difference!" he said to himself. And so he pulled his eldest daughter out from behind the throne. "Here she is," he pretended, and lifted her on to the Bear's back.

The Bear carried the eldest Princess deep into the snowy forest. Then he stopped. "Have you ever sat softer, have you ever seen clearer?" he growled.

"Oh yes!" boasted the eldest daughter. "My mother's lap is much softer. And from my father's castle I saw far clearer!"

"Well, you're not the right one then," roared the Bear, and tossed her off his back, and chased her all the way home. "I'll be back next Thursday for the true bride," he called.

Thursday came, and the soldiers loaded their cannons. As the Bear raced over the drawbridge, there was an enormous explosion. But the Bear's fur wasn't even marked. "I've come for my bride," he growled.

The King lifted his second daughter up on to the Bear's back. And the Bear carried her into the forest.

"Have you ever sat softer, have you ever seen clearer?" he growled.

"Ugggh!" sneered the second daughter. "My mother's lap is much softer. And from my father's castle I saw far clearer."

"You're not the right one then," roared the Bear, and chased her home. "I'll be back next Thursday for the true bride."

Thursday came, and the King stood on the drawbridge alone. The Bear charged towards him, with his mouth open and sharp teeth shining. The King was terrified, and called for his youngest daughter. "Take great care of her," said the King, "for she is my dearest." And he lifted her up on to the Bear's back.

The Bear carried her deep into the forest. Then he stopped. "Have you ever sat softer, have you ever seen clearer?" he growled.

"Never," whispered the youngest Princess, "no, never."

The Bear carried the Princess to a splendid palace.

"Everything here is yours," he said. "All you must do, is trust me."

That night the Princess slept in a bed, while the Bear lay by the fire. But in the middle of the night, the Princess was woken by a ripping sound. The Bear was digging his claws into his fur, and tearing at his skin. He pulled off the bearskin, and underneath was a man. He whispered kindly to the Princess, telling her not to be afraid. She listened to his voice, but it was too dark for her to see his face. And before dawn, he was back in the bearskin.

During the day he was a bear, but at night he was a man. A year passed, and the Princess got used to her changeable husband. Then, to her joy, she had a baby. But as soon as it was born, the Bear took the baby away, and she never saw it again. The next year she had a second child, but to her horror, the Bear took that away as well. In the third year, when her third child was taken, she felt as if her heart

would break. She longed to see her mother and father again, and asked the Bear if she could visit them. The Bear agreed, but he warned her, "Remember to trust me. For the moment you forget, the harm will already have been done."

The Princess travelled home, and was given a warm welcome by her family. Then she told her mother and father about her husband. "He is a bear during the day," she explained, "but at night he is a man. I had three children, and he has taken them all away."

"How terrible and cruel," said her mother. "He must be a monster. Does he have red eyes or fangs?"

"I don't know, Mother. I've never seen his face."

"Well, you must!" cried the Queen. "Take this candle and look at him. Then you will see what kind of beast you are married to."

Her father shook his head and said, "That will only do more harm than good."

But the Princess took the candle, and put it into her pocket.

When the Princess returned to the Bear's palace, she waited until he had taken off his bearskin, and was fast asleep. She wanted to know what he looked like –so much– that she quite forgot his warning. She lit the candle, and held it over his face. He was not a monster at all. He was very, very handsome. She held her breath and gazed at him

in wonder, leaning closer and closer. When suddenly, a drop of wax fell from the candle and splashed on to his forehead.

"Oh, Princess!" he cried, waking up with a start. "Why didn't you trust me? I am under a spell. In one more week, the spell would have been broken, and I would have been a man at last." The Princess gasped. "But the harm has already been done. Now I must leave you, and marry the terrible Troll Hag, who put the spell upon me, and be a bear forever." Then he pulled on his bearskin.

The Princess was desperate not to lose him, and flung herself on to his back. The Bear jumped out of the window and sped through the forest. The Princess clung to his fur, until her hands were as cold as ice, then she tumbled into the snow. When she awoke it was morning, and the Bear had gone. So she brushed the snow from her torn gown, and set off to find him.

The Princess scrambled through the forest all day. As dusk fell, she came to a little cottage. Outside was an old woman tending a fire. She had a long nose, a very long nose. It was so long, she was raking the ashes with it!

"Have you seen the White Bear King?" asked the Princess.

"He rushed by yesterday," replied the old woman. "You won't catch him tonight. Come in and rest with us." And she beckoned the Princess into a cosy cottage.

Inside was a little girl playing with a pair of golden scissors, snipping and clipping in the air. As she cut, lacy petticoats and dresses of silk and velvet appeared

out of nowhere. The little girl looked at the Princess's torn clothes, and at once snipped and clipped a warm, red, woollen shawl for her. The Princess wrapped herself in it gratefully.

"Granny," said the girl, "this lady needs the scissors more than I do, can I give them to her?"

"Of course," smiled the old woman.

So the Princess put the scissors into her pocket.

The next day, she walked and walked until she came to a second cottage. Outside was an old woman with an even longer nose. It was so long, she was digging holes in the snow, and planting seeds with it!

"Have you seen the White Bear King?" asked the Princess.

"He rushed by two days ago," replied the old woman. "You won't catch him tonight. Come in and rest with us."

Inside was a little girl playing with a golden cup. She tipped the cup this way and that, and whatever she wished to drink appeared out of nowhere. The little girl looked at the cold, tired Princess, and at once she tipped some piping hot potato broth for her. The Princess warmed her hands on the cup, and drank the soup gratefully.

"Granny," said the girl, "this lady needs the cup more than I do, can I give it to her?"

"Of course," beamed the old woman.

So the Princess put the cup into her pocket.

She walked until she came to a third cottage. Outside was an old woman with an even longer nose! It was so long, she was pulling up a bucket of water from the well with it!

"Have you seen the White Bear King?" asked the Princess.

"He rushed by three days ago. You won't catch him tonight. Come in and rest with us."

Inside was a little girl playing with a white cloth. She laid it out and said, "Cloth, spread thyself and deck thyself with every good dish." Suddenly, food appeared out of nowhere, completely covering the cloth. The Princess was hungry, and devoured a delicious feast.

"Granny," said the girl, "this lady needs the cloth more than I do, can I give it to her?"

"Of course," twinkled the old woman.

So the Princess put the cloth into her pocket.

The Princess walked so far that she came to the end of the path. There before her was a wall of shining crystal. It was a mountain, made of glass. The sheer wall stretched high into the sky, disappearing into the clouds. At the bottom was a little hut. The Princess peeped inside, and saw lots of ragged children, crying, "Mummy, I'm hungry!"

Their mother filled a saucepan with stones, put it on the fire, and said, "Hush, children, the potatoes will soon be done." The children stopped crying, and sat down to wait.

The Princess was shocked. "Why did you do that?" she asked.

"It deadens their hunger," sighed the mother. "I have nothing to give them, until their father comes home."

At once, the Princess pulled the cloth out of her pocket, and said, "Cloth, spread thyself and deck thyself with every good dish."

Suddenly the cloth was covered with roast meat, steaming potatoes, baked fish, buttery bread, hot pies and piles of sweet cakes. The children had never seen such a feast.

They ate and ate, and then they were thirsty. The Princess pulled out the golden cup and tipped and poured hot chocolate, lemonade, and a little nip of whisky for the mother. Then the Princess pulled out the scissors, and began snipping and cutting in the air. Dresses and shirts, trousers and capes, stockings and shoes, flew everywhere.

"How can I ever thank you?" said the mother.

"Well, I am looking for the White Bear King. Have you seen him?" asked the Princess.

"Oh, I saw him rush up the glass mountain a week ago. You won't get up there. Not even the birds can fly to the top."

At that, the Princess began to cry.

"Don't despair," said the mother kindly. "My husband is a blacksmith – perhaps he could make you some bear's claws. Then you could try to climb the mountain."

When the blacksmith returned, he spent all night hammering in his forge. He made two pairs of sharp pointed claws with strong leather straps.

The Princess buckled the claws on to her hands and knees, and began to climb the mountain: digging the claws into the glass and dragging herself up, until the hut was a tiny speck below. Digging the claws in and dragging herself up, until her arms ached, and her knees were red raw. Digging the claws in and dragging herself up, up, up, until she felt she could climb no more. Then suddenly, she came through the swirling clouds and reached the top.

There stood a dark castle, with lots of little trolls running around. They had red eyes, fat noses, hairy bellies and hairy feet.

"Have you seen the White Bear King?" asked the Princess.

"Oh yes! He's marrying our Mistress," chanted the trolls. "But no one's allowed to see him, except her."

The Princess walked over the drawbridge, to the castle gates. But the gates were locked fast. She just had to get inside. So she pulled the golden cup out of her pocket, and began to tip and pour sweet, sparkling, bubbly champagne. There was a rattle of keys, the gates creaked open, and there stood the terrible Troll Hag. She had a bony body and bony legs. She carried her head under her arm, and sticks and twigs stuck out of her neck. She had iron teeth, red eyes, and wiggling rats' tails for hair.

"OHH! Champagne!" shrieked the Troll Hag. "Just right for my wedding. How much is that cup?"

"It's not to be had for money," replied the Princess. "It's only to be had if I can spend a night with the White Bear King."

"Very well," cackled the Troll Hag. "But I must lull him to sleep first." And she snatched the cup.

That night the Princess was taken along winding passageways to the White Bear King's chamber. He was in his man's form, fast asleep. The Princess rushed to kiss him, but he did not open his eyes. She shook him, and spoke to him, but he would not wake up all night.

The next morning she sat by the gate and pulled the cloth out of her pocket.

"Cloth, spread thyself and deck thyself with a wedding cake."

A cake appeared, with white icing, three tiers, and a little statue of the Troll Hag with her head under her arm!

"OOOHHH! A wedding cake!" squawked the Troll Hag. "How much is that cloth?"

"It's not to be had for money," replied the Princess. "It's only to be had for a night with the White Bear King."

"As long as I lull him to sleep," said the Troll Hag, snatching the cloth.

That night the King was fast asleep again. The Princess stamped and shouted, begged and pleaded, but he did not hear her. But the troll guarding the bedroom door, heard everything!

The next morning the troll said to the White Bear, "Sir,

a girl was here last night, saying she loved you and that she climbed the glass mountain for you. If I were you, sir, I wouldn't drink the wine that Mistress gives you at supper. It's drugged!"

The Princess sat by the gate, and pulled the scissors out of her pocket. She snipped and clipped the most fabulous wedding dress, with ribbons and flounces and a special neck on one side for the Troll Hag's head!

"OOOOHHHHH! A bridal gown," screamed the Troll Hag. "How much are those scissors?"

"They're not to be had for money. They're only to be had for a night with the White Bear King."

"If I lull him to sleep," said the Troll Hag, snatching the scissors.

That night the King had supper with the Troll Hag. He was in his man's form, and had carefully tied a sponge under his chin. Instead of drinking the drugged wine, he let it trickle into the sponge. The Troll Hag was so busy feeding herself, she didn't notice. Then the King pretended to fall asleep, and the trolls carried him to his room, snoring.

But the Troll Hag sniffed the air. "I don't trust him," she scowled. "Bring me my sewing basket." She took out her longest, sharpest darning needle. "Let's see if you're really asleep!" And she stuck the needle into the King's arm. She pushed it through the skin, through the flesh, to the bone. She pushed it right through the marrow, and out the other side. The King didn't even flinch.

"Let her in," cried the Troll Hag. "He's asleep."

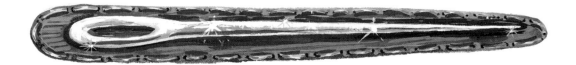

The Princess was downhearted, and walked slowly to the King's chamber. When she opened the door, there he was, sitting up in bed. She was so happy, she ran and hugged him.

"The suffering is not over," whispered the King. "Tomorrow I must marry the Troll Hag, and be a bear forever. The wedding procession will cross the drawbridge. If only we could cut the drawbridge ropes, the Troll Hag would die and the spell would be broken."

"I think I have just the thing in my pocket," said the Princess.

The only things left in her pocket were the claws. The Princess went to the drawbridge, and began to saw at the ropes with the sharp claws. When one claw was blunt, she used the next, sawing and scraping all night long, until the ropes were as fine as four strands of hair.

In the morning the Troll Hag was dressed in her wedding gown, with the little trolls as bridesmaids and pageboys. Behind them lumbered the White Bear King. As the trolls crossed the drawbridge, it began to shake. One by one, the trolls tumbled over the edge. Then there was an almighty crack, and the bridge broke. The terrible Troll Hag plummeted down the mountain. She fell crashing to the ground, and smashed into a thousand pieces!

There was only one troll left, and that was the kind guard. "Somebody has to be King," he said. And a very good King he was too!

The spell was broken. The White Bear's skin vanished, and he was wholly a man at last. He took the Princess into his arms, and suddenly they were at the bottom of the glass mountain. There, waiting to greet them with garlands of flowers, were the three old women and the three little girls.

"The suffering is over," twinkled the three old women. "Now, let us introduce you to your three own daughters."

The Princess looked at her three little girls in amazement, and felt she would burst with happiness. "Now I understand why you were taken from me," she said, hugging them joyfully. "So that you would help me find my true love again." And they all held hands and danced together in a ring.

Then the King, the Princess and their three daughters had a party. Everybody was invited, including you. The cloth was spread, and you ate whatever you liked. The cup was tipped, and you drank so much that you don't remember the party at all!

The End